DATE DUE			

The LION AND the STOAT

BY

PAUL O. ZELINSKY

BASED IN PART ON NATURAL HISTORY by PLINY the ELDER

GREENWILLOW BOOKS

NEW YORK

With love, for Grandma and Grandpa

Episodes I and II are based on anecdotes
from *Natural History* by Pliny the Elder.

Library of Congress Cataloging in Publication Data
Zelinsky, Paul O.
The lion and the stoat.
Summary: Two great artists, a lion and a stoat,
are in constant competition.
[1. Lions—Fiction.   2. Weasels—Fiction.
3. Artists—Fiction]   I. Pliny, the Elder.
Naturalis historia.   II. Title.
PZ7.Z3966Li   1984   [E]   83-16326
ISBN 0-688-02562-5
ISBN 0-688-02563-3 (lib. bdg.)

Far away in a small country, there lived two artists.

One of them was a stoat, the other a lion. They were both good painters; but the stoat was better— at least according to the stoat.

And the lion thought, "I can paint circles around that stoat."

He challenged the stoat to a contest. "Meet me in the market square at noon, two weeks from today," he told the stoat. "Each of us will bring a painting, and the public will be the judge."

The stoat agreed.

The lion went home and worked like an ox for the next two weeks. When he finished, he said, "It's small but it's perfect."

The stoat put the last touches to his painting. "That's it," he said. "It couldn't be better."

On the day of the contest the whole town
assembled at the marketplace.

The two paintings were hung on a wall,
each covered by a velvet curtain.

"I will show my painting first," said the lion, and he drew back the curtain. The crowd began to clap. Suddenly some sparrows flew down to the painting and began to peck at the grapes.

"I win!" roared the lion. "My painting looks so real it has even fooled the birds! Can you top that, Stoat? Let's see what is behind that curtain of yours."

The stoat cleared his throat. "My dear Lion," he said, "there is no curtain. What you see is my painting of a velvet curtain. Your still life may have fooled the birds, but my painting has fooled you."

The crowd cheered. The lion broke three paintbrushes over his knee, as the stoat was declared the winner.

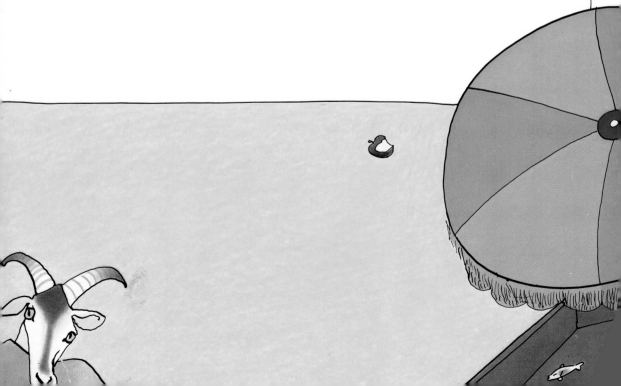

oon after, the stoat built himself a large shed on
the outskirts of town.

"Come visit my new studio," he said to the lion.

"I am much too busy," the lion replied. He was still angry over the stoat's victory. But as the day went on, his curiosity grew. And first thing the next morning he took a long walk right to the stoat's studio.

The stoat was not at home, but the door was un–
locked and the lion walked in.

There was little in the room but a table on which lay a
palette, tubes of paint, and a can of brushes. Next to the

table stood an easel holding a blank white canvas.

"This is private property!" snapped a turtle who was sitting under the table. "What are you doing here? Kindly remove yourself."

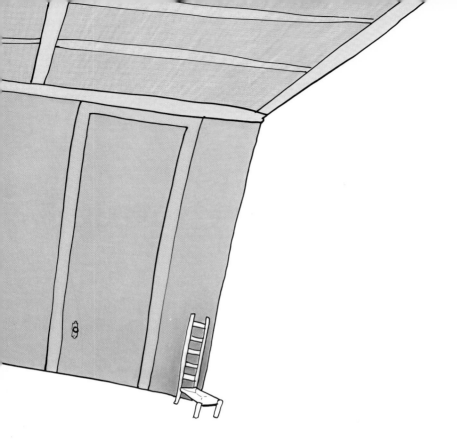

The lion growled. "Do you know whom you are talking to?" He picked up a brush, squeezed some paint on it, and said, "Tell your artist to look at this canvas— he will know who was here." Then he painted a very thin, straight line across the exact middle of the canvas, and left.

Soon the stoat came home. "Thanks for keeping an eye on the place," he said to the turtle. Then he saw the canvas. "What is this?" he asked.

"Some fellow was here," said the turtle. "He said you'd know who it was when you saw the canvas."

"Ah, yes," said the stoat. "And if I know him, he'll be back. Tell him, when he comes, that there is a message for him on the canvas."

The stoat dipped a brush in a different color and painted another, even thinner line over the one the lion had made. It cut the first line right through the middle. Then he went out again.

That very afternoon the lion returned.

"There's a message for you on the canvas," said the turtle.

The lion looked at the canvas. "That's not bad," he said. "However—" and he painted a third line over the other two. It was so thin it was almost invisible: it cut both the other lines straight through the middle. The lion returned to town smiling to himself.

When the stoat came home, he went right to the canvas, looked at it, and whistled.

"Nobody can split that line," he said.

He hurried into town and found the lion in the cafe eating dinner.

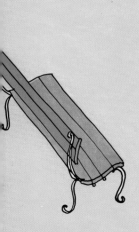

"I give up," the stoat said. "You've painted the finest line I have ever seen."

"Thank you," said the lion. "I do believe it may be the finest line ever painted. Won't you join me for dinner?" And the stoat did.

Before dinner was over, they had decided to give the painting to the National Museum, where it hangs to this day. They called it "The Three Lines," because unless you look carefully, you may think there is only one.

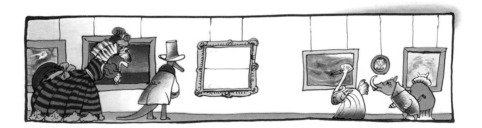

The next year, the Town Hall, which was very old, collapsed.

A new one was quickly built. It had a big, empty wall in the Town Council meeting room.

"We need a painting for this wall," the Council decided when it met. A councilbird raised his wing. "We have two fine painters in this town, the lion and the stoat," he said. "Why don't we commission one of them to do a painting?"

"Let the lion and the stoat each make a painting," the mayor suggested. "Something impressive. Then we can choose the better one."

The Council approved and both artists agreed to the plan.

The lion thought, "I will surely win this one. All I need is the right subject." The lion had many ideas, but none of them seemed good enough.

The stoat thought, "Mine has got to be the best." But should he paint this, or that?

Nothing seemed quite right, until . . .

Both artists worked day and night for weeks.

On the day the choice was to be made, a crowd
gathered at the new Town Hall. The mayor stood at the
top of the steps to greet the artists. As the lion and the

stoat arrived with their paintings, a flock of sparrows
flew over the crowd. "Watch out if it's grapes," one of
them piped up. "You'll hurt your beaks."

The mayor uncovered the first painting. The crowd gasped. It was a picture of a lion. It was the lion himself.

"A perfect likeness," said the mayor, "though not exactly what we had expected."

Then she uncovered the stoat's painting. It was a picture of a stoat. It was the stoat himself. "Another perfect likeness," said the mayor. "Though not exactly what we had expected," she repeated.

"But both are fine paintings. Indeed," she said, "I have never seen a better painting of a lion or a stoat. Two pictures of two great artists, painted by two great artists! Let us hang both pictures, one next to the other."

"Yes!" voted the Council unanimously.

The crowd clapped and cheered.

"Well, Stoat," said the lion, "are you satisfied?"

"In fact," the stoat replied, "I am delighted."

"So am I," said the lion. "Delighted, but hungry. Shall we celebrate our victory with a nice lunch?"

"Yes, indeed," replied the stoat. "And by the way,

may I suggest something? Let's forget about contests from now on."

"Agreed," said the lion.

And off they went to eat.